Published by Calithumpian Press, LLC
CalithumpianPress.com

Book designed by Paul Williams and edited by Lisa Pliscou.

The text in this book is Neutraface by House Industries.
The font for the title is Elroy. We also used a fun font called
Playtime With Hot Toddies.

First Edition – 2016

Library of Congress Control Number: 2016905172
Cataloging-In-Publication Data available

ISBN: 978-0-9886341-9-0

Printed in the United States of America
by Phoenix Color, Hagerstown, Maryland.

10 9 8 7 6 5 4 3 2 1 ... up, up, and away!

www.KeeKeesBigAdventures.com
Facebook: KeeKee's Big Adventures
Twitter: @KeeKeeAdventure

This great adventure began
on a KLM Airlines flight in 2006
moving to the wonderful city of Amsterdam
with the real-life KeeKee.
Amsterdam was our home for four years,
and our travels across Europe led us
on the path to launching KeeKee's Big Adventures.
We dedicate this book to those inspirations.

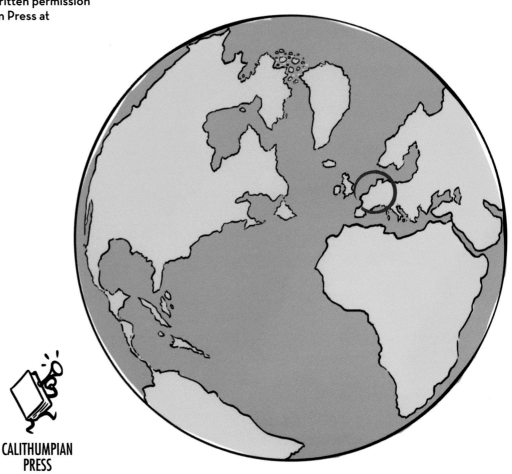

CALITHUMPIAN
PRESS

KeeKee's Big Adventures

TM

in Amsterdam, Netherlands

Story by Shannon Jones

Illustrations by Casey Uhelski

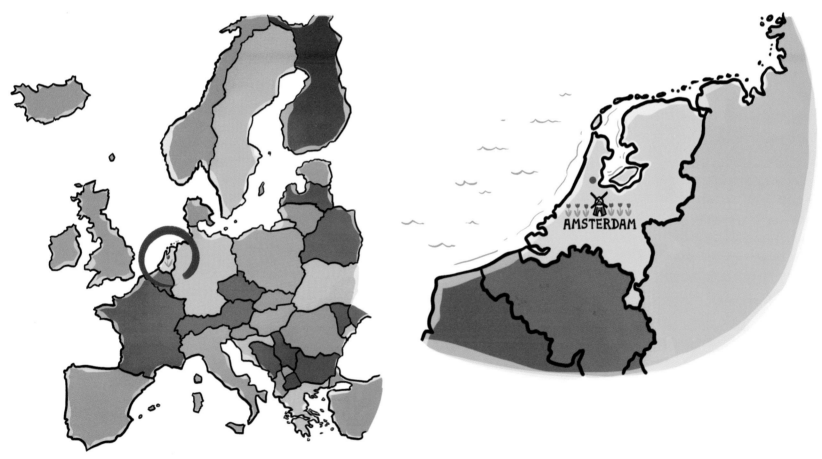

AMSTERDAM

"*Goedemorgen!* Good morning!" said Jasper.
"*Welkom* to the Netherlands!"

"Thank you! *Dank u wel!*" answered KeeKee.

"What brings
you to Holland?"
Jasper asked.

"Wow! A real Dutch windmill," said KeeKee.

"Windmills are factories that turn wind into power," explained Jasper. "Let's go see what's happening inside."

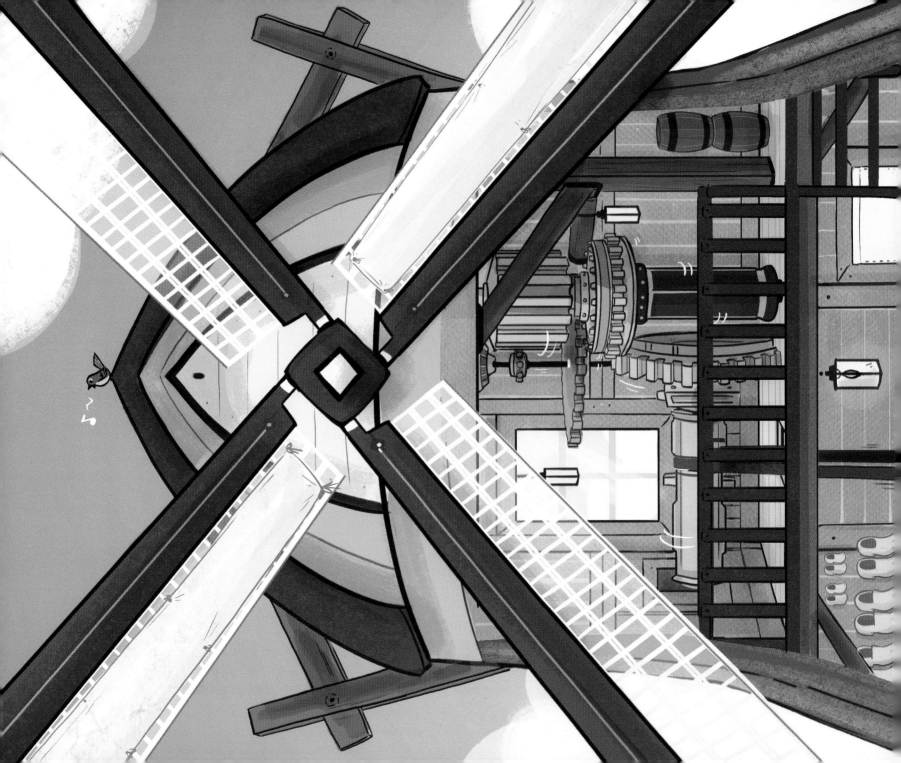

KeeKee and Jasper watched *klompen* – wooden shoes – being made. "They're a tradition here in Holland," Jasper told KeeKee. "And they're still worn today by gardeners, farmers, and road workers."

"Klompen are great for stompin'!" laughed KeeKee.

klomp
klomp

"Let's get these tulips to my friend Marijn."

"The *Bloemenmarkt* is the city's famous flower market. All these stalls are actually floating in the canal. There's nothing else like it in the world," said Jasper.

"The butcher, the baker, and the catnip maker," said KeeKee.

And the Kick & Faas *Kaas* Shop," said Jasper. *Kaas* means cheese. Let's try our famous *Gouda* cheese."

"Yum, this sure is good-a!" giggled KeeKee.

And that was only the beginning! There were more stops on their exciting tasting tour of the town.

They had *haring*...

...*pannenkoeken* and *poffertjes*...

eet smakelijk

enjoy the meal

...*kroket* and *friet*,
and *stroopwafel*, too!

"And now... your canal cruise!"
announced Jasper.

"I'm ready to go when you are!" said KeeKee.

"We'll take my little boat, down there," Jasper said.
"This boat stays docked. It's my home – my houseboat."

"How cool is this? You get to live in a house that floats! And it's just as big as a regular house."

Amsterdam has more canals
than any other city in the world.

The buildings along them
are houses and shops.

Long ago, the canals
were used as highways
for boats to deliver supplies.

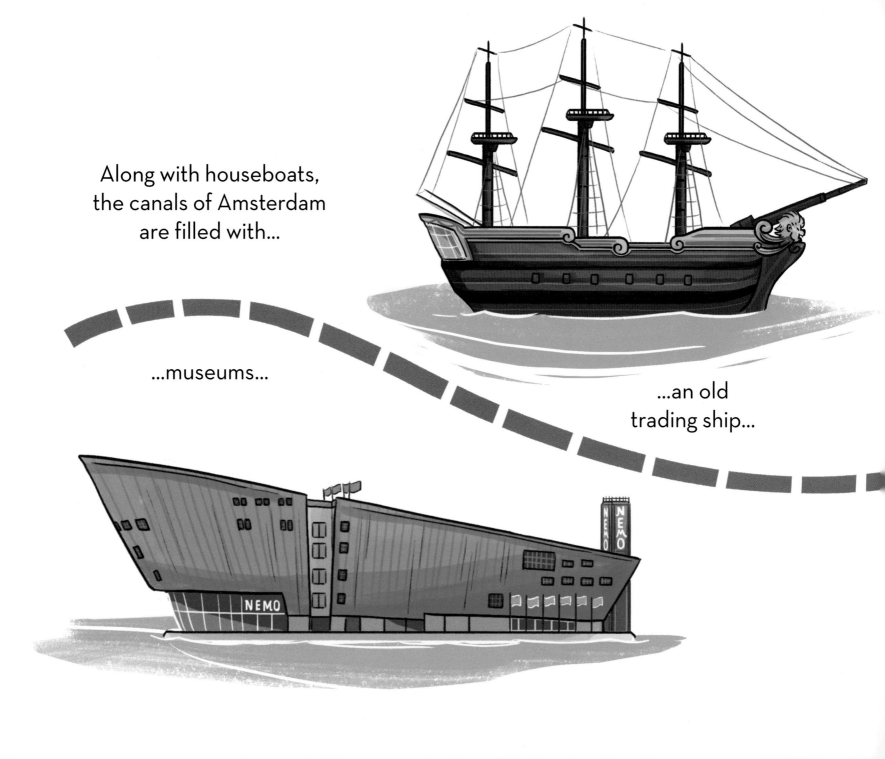

Along with houseboats,
the canals of Amsterdam
are filled with...

...museums...

...an old
trading ship...

There's even a boat
where only cats live,
De Poezenboot!

...and a floating
Chinese restaurant.

"On nice days, the canals
can get pretty busy," Jasper said.

"Boat jam!" said KeeKee.
"Let's get out of here."

Hallo, Marijn,
Kick, and Faas!

"Goedenavond!
Good evening, KeeKee
and Jasper!" called Marijn.
"Come join us on the terrace."

Pronunciation Guide & Glossary

Words & Phrases

Alstublieft	(AHLST-ew-bleeft)	Please
Bedankt	(beh-dankt)	Thank you
Dag	(dakh)	Goodbye
Dank je	(dahnk yuh)	Thank you
Dank u wel	(dahnk ew vehl)	Thank you very much
Doei	(DOO-wee)	Bye
Eet smakelijk	(ATE SMAH-kuh-luhk)	Enjoy the meal
Fietsen	(FEET-sen)	Bicycles
Friet	(freet)	Dutch french fries
Gezellig	(heh-ZEH-lick)	Cozy and friendly environment
Goedenavond	(KHOO-duh-NAH-vond)	Good evening
Goedemorgen	(KHOO-duh-MAWR-ghuh)	Good morning
Graag gedaan	(GRAHG guh-DAHN)	You're welcome
Haring	(HAR-ring)	Herring fish
Hallo/Hoi	(HAH-low / Hoy)	Hello
Hoera	(hoo-RAH)	Hooray
Ja	(yah)	Yes
Kaas	(kahs)	Cheese
Katten	(caht-TEN)	Cats
Klompen	(klom-PEN)	Wooden shoes; clogs
Kroket	(crow-KET)	Dutch croquette
Lekker	(leh-KER)	Yummy
Miauw	(me-YOW)	Meow
Mooi	(moy)	Beautiful
Pannekoeken	(pan-nuh-KOOK-en)	Dutch pancakes
Poffertjes	(poefer-tjes)	Dutch beignets
Stroopwafel	(stroep-VAH-fel)	thin waffles with syrup in between
Tot ziens	(toat zeens)	So long; see you later
Welkom	(vell-COME)	Welcome

Places

Holland - The Netherlands is made up of 12 provinces; two of them are North and South Holland. In these two provinces are the country's main cities, including Amsterdam.

Tulip Fields - Just outside Amsterdam, is the famous *bollenstreek* – bulb-growing region – with miles of colorful flower fields.

Munttoren/Mint Tower - In the 1600s, this tall clock tower near the Flower Market briefly housed the city's mint, where money was made.

Bloemenmarkt - The world's only floating flower market. It first opened in 1862. Flowers would arrive every day from the countryside by boat.

Amstel River - Amsterdam was founded on the banks of this river as a fishing village. It was dammed in 1222, thus leading to the city's name.

Grachtengordel - The famous semicircle of canals around the city. There are over 165 canals, more than in Venice or any other city in the world.

East Indiaman Amsterdam - A full-scale replica of a Dutch East India Company trading ship that sank on its first voyage in 1749.

De Poezenboot/The Cat Boat - A floating shelter for stray cats on the Singel Canal.

NEMO - Amsterdam's science museum resembles a ship docked in the harbor.

Rijksmuseum - The National Museum is home to some of the world's greatest Dutch art, including *The Night Watch* by Rembrandt and *The Milkmaid* by Vermeer.

Magere Brug/Skinny Bridge - Of the city's 1,200 bridges, this wooden drawbridge is one of the most famous.